SUPERSTAR WATCH

created by
GERTRUDE CHANDLER WARNER

Illustrated by Robert Papp

Albert Whitman & Company
Chicago, Illinois

Contents

SUPERSTAR WATCH

CHAPTER 1

An Exciting Opportunity

The Aldens were sitting in front of the Greenfield Ice Cream Café.

"You are the best brother ever. Thank you, Henry," six-year-old Benny said, rubbing his tummy. Henry had taken Benny and their two sisters, Jessie and Violet, out for a bike ride and a treat. Now the four children sat together quietly enjoying their ice cream cones.

The calm was suddenly broken. "Help me!" a voice called. It was Josh Greene, their neighbor. He went soaring past on his bike.

"I can't stop!" Josh called. "I think my brakes are out!" His bike was going fast.

The Aldens looked at each other. A split second later they were all running for their bikes.

Henry zoomed down the street on his mountain bike. "Hold on tight!" he shouted to Josh.

"We're coming!" twelve-year-old Jessie yelled. She and Violet and Benny wanted to help Josh too.

"You can't slow down at all?" Violet called out. She was ten and she rode her purple beach cruiser as fast as she could.

"No," Josh called back. "I think I'm going to crash!"

Brinnnggg went the bell of Benny's bike. "I'll save you!" Benny said. His training wheels scraped against the sidewalk as he tried to catch up.

"You're going to have to jump, Josh!" Henry yelled. He knew there was a steep slope ahead. If Josh went downhill, it would be even harder to stop.

"Josh, head toward the park," Jessie called. "If you have to crash, at least it'll be on grass."

Josh nodded. Instead of shooting straight towards the hill, he made a left on Main Street. The park was only a block away, near the town square.

Henry, Jessie, Violet, and Benny all stopped at the edge of the park. But Josh's bike jumped the sidewalk and kept on going.

In a swift, daring move, Josh leapt off his bike and rolled safely onto a grassy patch by the playground. Without a rider, the old bike kept on going until it finally slammed into a tree. Josh's bike tipped over in the dirt.

The Aldens left their bikes and went running.

"I'm fine," Josh told them. He got up and wiped loose grass off his jeans. "How's my bike?"

"Oh dear," Violet said, as she saw the damage.

The bike's frame was bent. Both tires had popped.

"Bad news, Josh. Your bike is dead. D-E-A-D." Jessie said.

"What am I going to do?" Josh groaned. "I need my bike to do my paper route." Josh had a messenger bag on his back. "I was making deliveries when my brakes gave out." The bag was half full with the afternoon's newspapers. "If I don't have my bike, I can't work." Josh sighed.

Jessie put an arm around Josh's shoulders. "Let's take it to the bike repair shop. I bet they'll know how to fix it."

The Aldens gathered their bikes and walked along with Josh. His bike's flat tires made a *clump, clomp* sound along the sidewalk.

When they got to Jim's Bike Shop, Josh looked at the shiny new bikes.

"I wish I could buy a new bike," he said. "But I don't know how I can even pay for repairs."

"Maybe it won't cost that much," Henry said. "Let's go see what Jim says."

Henry and Josh went to the back of the store.

"I'll call Grandfather and tell him we'll be

home a little later than we planned," Jessie said. "I don't want him to worry."

Henry, Jessie, Violet, and Benny lived with their grandfather. After their parents died, they ran away and hid in a railroad boxcar. They'd heard that Grandfather was mean and even though they'd never met him, they were afraid. The boxcar became their home. They even found a dog in the woods, took him in, and called him Watch.

When Grandfather located them, it turned out that he wasn't mean at all. They gladly went to live with him. Watch went, too. Even the boxcar went to Grandfather's house. Now it was a clubhouse in the backyard.

While they waited for Josh and Henry, Benny and Violet looked at the new bikes. Jessie began reading flyers posted on the wall.

At last Henry and Josh came back. Josh looked crushed.

"It's going to cost about a hundred dollars to fix my bike," he said. He put his head in his hands. "I don't know what to do. I don't have that much!"

"I wish we could help," Henry said.

"Maybe we could raise money with a car wash," Violet suggested.

"A bake sale would be better," Benny said. He and Violet came over to Jim's front desk. "I love bake sales!" Benny went on. "So many yummy things to eat."

"Benny might eat everything at a bake sale before any customers arrived." Violet laughed, gently teasing her brother.

"Hold on. I have an even better idea!" Jessie announced. She pointed at a bright green flyer on Jim's bulletin board. "I know how we can help Josh pay for his bike repairs."

Violet read the sign out loud: "Wundermutt Dog Food is looking for a new Wundermutt TV star."

Jessie pointed to some small writing at the bottom of the flyer. It read: PRIZE MONEY WILL BE AWARDED.

"Fame and fortune!" Benny said. "Our dog, Watch, will take the fame," he told Josh. "And you can have the fortune!"

Henry leaned in to look at the poster.

"The auditions are being held today at the Greenfield Mall." Benny looked confused so Henry explained, "An audition is a try-out. The dogs will do all kinds of tests and the best dog will win."

"The flyer says that the auditions begin at two o'clock." Jessie said. "It's already one now. We'd better hurry."

"Let's go!" Benny exclaimed. "Watch is so awesome! He's sure to win! He'll be a star, just like my favorite TV dog, Ninja! Let's do it!"

"Do you think the Wundermutt company would give you a hundred dollars?" Josh asked.

"We won't know unless we try," Henry said. "While Watch auditions, you can borrow my bike for a of couple days to do your paper route."

"Thank you so much, Henry." Josh's eyes were now much brighter and happier. "I sure hope Watch gets the commercial."

"Cross your fingers," Henry told Josh. "And keep them crossed."

"It'll be hard to deliver papers with my fingers crossed," Josh said with a laugh. "But I'll do my best."

"Watch will do his best, too," Benny said.

* * * *

"Grandfather, we're home!" Jessie announced. Then she said to the others, "Violet, please get Watch's brush. Benny, you are in charge of his leash."

Watch came bounding into the room at the sound of Jessie's voice.

"Where's the fire?" Grandfather asked, coming out of his study.

"Watch is going to be on TV," Violet said.

"A big star!" Benny held out his hands to show just how big.

Then, Benny told Grandfather the whole story. He was so excited he said it all without taking a single breath.

"Whoa," Grandfather said, putting out a hand towards Benny. "Slow down. What's this about Josh Greene crashing in the park?"

"He's fine. He wasn't hurt," Henry said.

"We're going to give him the prize money," Violet added.

"Prize money?" Grandfather asked. "What prize money? I thought this was about Watch."

Jessie hooked Watch's leash to his collar. "We can explain on the way to the mall."

Grandfather looked puzzled. "The mall?" he asked.

"Can you please take us there?" Henry asked.

"You promise you'll explain on the way?" Grandfather replied.

Henry nodded. "Every single detail," he agreed.

"All right then," Grandfather said, pulling out his car keys.

"Are you ready to be a superstar, Watch?" Benny asked.

CHAPTER 2

A Long Line

"Hold hands, Benny." Jessie reached out to take his hand in hers. "We have to stick together. This place is really crowded."

"It looks like every dog owner in town is at the mall today," Henry said. In the center courtyard of the mall, there was a long and winding line of people and pets that had shown up for the dog audition.

"This is like waiting for a ride at an amusement park in the middle of summer," Violet said.

They walked to find the end of the line. They were almost there when Benny suddenly shouted, "Ninja!" He yanked his hand out of Jessie's.

"Ninja, the TV star?" Jessie asked. She saw Benny dashing towards a tall, thin man with a dog. The dog was a black Labrador on a rhinestone-studded leash. Henry, who was leading Watch, and Violet hurried over to see what the fuss was about.

"Why would Ninja be here in Greenfield?" Violet wondered. "I don't think it could be him, Benny."

"I am a million percent sure. That is definitely Ninja," Benny said, "I'd know him anywhere!"

Benny went up to the dog's owner. "Hi. I've seen every episode of 'Ninja at Night.' It's my favorite show. Ninja is my hero," Benny said. "Can I pet Ninja? Please?"

The black lab looked up at Benny, his tail wagging eagerly.

"No!" the man said sternly. "No one pets Ninja. He is preparing for his audition and must not be disturbed." The man pulled Ninja away from Benny. "He needs to concentrate."

Ninja stopped wagging his tail and lowered his head.

"I cannot believe we have to audition like regular folk," the man muttered loud enough so that everyone around could hear. "This is outrageous. Ninja is a star." The man stuck his nose in the air, then turned his back on the Aldens.

"Come on, Benny," Jessie said, taking her brother's hand back in hers. She gave it a squeeze.

"We'd better get in line anyway," Henry said. "Even more dogs have arrived since we first got here."

"I feel bad for Ninja," Violet said as they led Watch through the crowd. "That dog looked like he wanted to be petted."

Benny walked along with the others. He dragged his feet sadly.

The children took their place in line. At exactly two o'clock, a woman in a suit stepped up onto a small platform with a microphone in the middle of the mall courtyard. A younger blonde woman followed her carrying a clipboard.

"Testing. One. Two. Three. Attention everyone." The woman in the suit spoke. A hush fell over the crowd. Benny looked down to make sure Watch was listening. His terrier ears were standing up at attention.

"Good dog," Benny whispered. He scratched Watch behind the ears.

"Welcome. My name is Margaret Werner. I am the Advertising Manager for the Wundermutt Company. Let me begin by telling you how thrilled we are that so many dogs and their owners came to the mall today." The woman gave a small smile. "Now, I must let you know that the Wundermutt Company has decided that we are looking for a larger dog."

Some people in the crowd began to mutter.

"I am so sorry," Ms. Werner told them. "But if your dog is shorter than this," she put her hand by her knee, "it will not be allowed to audition today. Maybe another day we will come back looking for a smaller dog. Thank you so much for supporting the Wundermutt Company and our delicious dog food and other products."

A number of people and their small dogs left the audition. The Alden children and Watch were able to move up in line.

"Watch is just the right size!" Benny said.

"So far, so good," Henry agreed.

Ms. Werner spoke again. "We are also looking for a dog that is not too skinny. Too fat. Or too old. The dog must be healthy and well trained."

More people and their dogs left the line. The Alden children could hear some people sigh sadly as they left.

"Watch still fits," Violet said.

"Whew," Jessie breathed in relief. "I think he's got a really good chance! He's certainly well trained and can do a lot of great tricks."

Henry took a quick count. "There are now only about fifty people and their dogs left in line."

Benny reached into his pocket and pulled out a lucky penny. "Here," he told Henry, "rub it for luck."

Henry smiled and took the penny. He ran his finger over Lincoln's face, then handed it back.

Benny grinned. He put his good luck charm back into his pocket.

Ms. Werner continued, "In just a few minutes, I will go down the line and take a close look at each dog. If your dog has the right look for the commercial, I will give it a bowl of our food to snack on. All other dogs will be sent home."

"A snack!" Benny exclaimed. "I wish they had a snack for the dog owners, too." His brother and sisters all smiled. Benny had a bottomless appetite.

The Alden children were now close to the platform where Ms. Werner and the blonde woman stood. They watched as Ms. Werner stepped off the platform. "Lisa," she said to the blonde woman, "I'm going to get the food and bowls. You stay here and hand out coupons."

Lisa didn't look happy about her job. She grumbled as she sat down behind the coupon table.

A few minutes later, the Aldens saw Ms. Werner return with a pushcart. She had a big bag of Wundermutt dog food and a stack of plastic souvenir dog bowls. She started at the head of the line and poured a bowl of food for a very pretty golden retriever.

But the next two dogs in line did not get food. "I'm so sorry. Yours are not the kind of dogs we are looking for today. Lisa will give you some coupons for our dog food on your way out," Ms. Werner told the owners.

"Yours gets a snack," Ms. Werner said, and gave food to another dog as she continued down the line.

Benny put his hand in his pocket and rubbed his lucky penny again. "I sure hope Watch gets food instead of getting sent home," he told Violet.

"Me, too," Violet agreed. Benny handed her the penny. She rubbed it and handed it back.

"Yippee for Ninja!" Benny said happily when he saw the black Lab get a bowl of food.

But Ninja's owner didn't like being stuck in line. "My dog is a star," he said. "He should have simply been given the role."

Ms. Werner shook her head. "As I already told you, your dog must try out just like everyone else's."

"Hmph," said Ninja's owner. Ms. Werner turned away.

Ms. Werner continued down the line. When she finally got to Watch, she took a few extra seconds studying him.

Benny squeezed his penny tight. Jessie crossed her fingers. Violet was so nervous, she closed her eyes. Henry tapped his toe against the floor.

After what seemed like a very long time, Ms. Werner said, "A snack for your terrier." She poured Watch a big bowl of food.

"Whew!" The Aldens all breathed huge sighs of relief. Watch had made it through the first round of the audition!

Ms. Werner set the bowl down in front of Watch. Jessie noticed the scent of a strong perfume.

"Do you smell flowers?" she asked her brothers and sister as Ms. Werner moved off to check out the next dog.

"Not flowers." Henry lifted his nose and took a long sniff. "It's more like lemons."

"Achoo," Benny sneezed. "Whatever it is, it's making me sneezy!"

"I'm trying to remember exactly where I've smelled that odor before." Violet stood quietly thinking for a while. "I know!" she declared at last. "That fragrance isn't flowers or lemons. It's citronella."

"Citron...what?" Benny asked, rubbing his nose and sneezing again.

"Citronella," Violet said. "It's a lemony, flowery smelling oil that's put in candles and sprays. It keeps bugs away."

"Maybe Ms. Werner is wearing a new citronella perfume—perfect for summer time," Jessie said with a laugh. "Whatever it is, I like it." Jessie sniffed and added, "The scent sure does last a long time. I can still smell it even though she's all the way down near the end of the line now."

"Hmm," Violet said, pinching her lips together and tugging at her long brown pigtails.

"What are you thinking?" Henry asked his sister.

"I don't know yet," Violet replied. "But something doesn't feel quite right."

"I was thinking that too, but not about the citronella." Jessie said. "I was wondering why a big star like Ninja needs to audition for this commercial. What's a Hollywood dog doing in our little town of Greenfield?"

"Want to know what I'm wondering?" Benny asked his siblings.

"What?" Henry, Violet, and Jessie asked at once.

Benny pointed at Watch who was sniffing the bowl of dog food in front of him. "Wundermutt food is Watch's favorite. But he's not eating it. Why not?" Benny took a step back and looked down the line. "Look," he told his brother and sisters. "None of the dogs are eating the food."

Jessie, Henry, and Violet glanced up and down the audition line. "Benny is right," Jessie said. "Not even one dog in the whole line is eating the food. The bowls are all still full."

"Strange," Henry said, rubbing his chin. "Most dogs will eat almost anything... It looks like we've stumbled onto a mystery."

CHAPTER 3

Audition Action

Chomp. Chomp. Chomp.

Suddenly the Aldens could hear the unmistakable sound of a dog eating. The children looked at each other. The sound was coming from near the end of the line.

"Hold on!" Jessie said. "That dog is eating the food." Jessie pointed to a black and white speckled sheepdog. A boy about Jessie's age was standing with the dog as it chomped away at his bowl of food.

"Why is that dog the only one in the

whole line eating the food?" Henry wanted
to know.

"Maybe the other dogs aren't hungry,"
Violet suggested.

"But Violet, they're *dogs*," Benny said.
"Grandfather once told me that dogs are
always a little hungry." He patted his tummy
and added, "Sometimes, I think *I* might be
part dog."

Henry and Violet laughed.

"Woof," Jessie teased, patting him on the
head.

From where they stood, the Aldens could
hear Ms. Werner talking to the boy with the
speckled dog.

"What is your name?" Ms. Werner asked.

"Dante Oliver," the boy replied. "And this
is Buffalo."

Benny giggled and whispered to Violet,
"That dog looks nothing like a buffalo."

"Well, Buffalo sure seems to be a nice dog,"
Ms. Werner said kindly to Dante. She put
out her hand and Buffalo licked it. Suddenly
Buffalo leapt forward. He pulled against his

leash and tried to get closer to Ms. Werner.

"Down," she said firmly, stepping away. "I'm going to put a star next to Buffalo's name," Ms. Werner told Dante. "We're going to keep an eye on your dog." Then she walked away.

"Oh no," Benny said to his siblings, "Ms. Werner already likes Buffalo best of all because he ate the Wundermutt food!"

"Don't worry," Jessie assured her little brother. "The auditions have barely begun."

Twenty dogs and their owners had made it through the first round. Ms. Werner and Lisa led them all to a special room in the mall reserved for the Wundermutt Company.

It was a large room. On one side there was an obstacle course, which was a little path with things for a dog to jump over or through—a wooden log, a small bench, a hoop. At the end of the course was a tall slide with thick stairs. On the other side of the room was a small stage with a set made up to look like a kitchen. Finally, at the back of the room, there was a little desk, a table with a coffee pot on it, and a few chairs. It looked like a makeshift office.

"Now we will pick the top three dogs," Ms. Werner told everyone. "All the dogs will have to do a few tricks—lie down, play dead, roll over, fetch, and bark."

When it was Watch's turn to do the tricks, he did everything right! He lay down like a carpet and didn't move. He played dead very well, and he rolled like a log, over and over until Jessie told him to stop. Watch jumped high to catch a ball in his mouth before returning it to Ms. Werner. And best of all, when Jessie told Watch to speak, he barked, loud and sharp.

"You sure trained him well," Henry told Jessie. She beamed happily.

Watch rested while the Aldens watched the other dogs. Ms. Werner and Lisa watched the tricks carefully and Lisa wrote notes on her clipboard.

Benny giggled when a big black dog walked across the room on her back legs, an extra trick. "She looks like a bear!" Benny said.

Another dog they watched could easily fetch the ball, but wouldn't give it back to Ms. Werner. After a few tries, Ms. Werner gave up and walked off.

Buffalo went next. He played dead pretty well, but didn't stay dead very long. He fetched a ball, but didn't catch it in the air. Instead, he waited until it stopped rolling, slowly got the ball, and very slowly brought it back.

"I think that Buffalo is part dog and part turtle," Benny said.

Ms. Werner whispered to Lisa, who wrote on her clipboard. Buffalo's turn was over.

"Oh look! There's Lucky," Violet said, recognizing the next dog. Lucky's owner, Samantha Fine, was in Violet's class at school. Lucky did very well at all the tricks.

"Lucky's good," Henry said, "but I think Watch is just as good."

Finally all the dogs had finished their tricks. Lisa tucked the clipboard under her arm and followed Ms. Werner out of the room.

"Ninja was really good, huh?" Benny said

while they waited. "Did you see him catch that ball Ms. Werner threw? That was way better than a regular fetch! I knew Ninja could jump super high. He does it on TV all the time." Benny loved seeing his hero do tricks.

"I wonder who they'll choose for the next round," Henry said.

The dog owners grew suddenly quiet as Ms. Werner and Lisa returned. There was a man with them. He was heavyset and bald.

Henry heard Ms. Werner say, "I still think it's crazy that company employees can't enter their dogs in the audition."

"Rules are rules," the man said firmly. "I don't want to discuss it again."

Ms. Werner pinched her lips together. Then she introduced the man to everyone in the room. "This is the owner of the Wundermutt Company, Mr. Lillipool," she said. "The search for a new Wundermutt star was his idea."

"And a fine idea it was," Mr. Lillipool said with a wide grin. He walked around, petting dogs and greeting everyone.

"Hello, children," Mr. Lillipool said to the Aldens. "Who is this?" he asked, bending low to scratch Watch beneath his collar. Watch immediately dropped to the floor and rolled on his back, wanting his belly to be scratched, too.

Mr. Lillipool laughed. His deep chuckle filled the room. "What a wonderful dog!" he exclaimed. He wished the Aldens good luck and then went off to look at the other dogs. They watched the way Mr. Lillipool petted each dog. "He sure loves dogs," Henry said.

When Mr. Lillipool was finished, Ms. Werner walked him to the door. They stood near the entrance whispering for a moment or two. At last Mr. Lillipool left and Ms. Werner turned to the group.

She clapped her hands and announced: "Our final three dogs are…"

Benny and Henry held their breath.

"Ninja," Ms. Werner said.

Ninja's owner raised his eyebrows. "Well, that's no surprise!" he said.

Jessie and Violet held their breath, too, as they waited to hear the next name.

"Watch," Ms. Werner said. The Aldens all exhaled at the same time.

"Whew!" Jessie said. She wanted to cheer, but there was one more name to be called.

"And our last finalist is," Ms. Werner paused. Finally she called out: "Buffalo."

"*Buffalo?*" Henry wondered.

Dante, Buffalo's owner, nodded at Ms. Werner. He didn't cheer or shout. Henry noticed that Dante didn't even smile. "I don't think Dante's very excited that Buffalo was picked," Henry said to Jessie. "I wonder why."

"It's like he knew Buffalo would make it all along," Jessie said.

Henry was about to say something more, but Ms. Werner interrupted.

"Thank you to everyone who tried out today. Please help yourselves to some Wundermutt dog food coupons on your way out," Ms. Werner told the crowd. She and Lisa stood near the door, saying good-bye to the other dog owners and handing out coupons.

"I don't understand how Buffalo got picked. He did all the tricks, but lots of dogs did better," Jessie said.

Violet went over to her friend Samantha and gave her a hug. "Your dog was really good," she told her.

"We did our best," Samantha replied, petting Lucky's head. "But if you ask me, Watch should get the commercial. He was amazing." Samantha glanced over at Dante and Buffalo. "Buffalo didn't do very well, did he?" she asked. "I don't understand why he gets to stay."

The Aldens waved good-bye to Samantha and Lucky and watched them leave.

Then Benny said, "I have two questions about Buffalo."

"What are they, Benny?" Henry asked.

"Number one," Benny held up one finger. "Why is he the only dog who ate the food? And number two," Benny held up a second finger. "Why does Buffalo get to stay when he didn't do very well in the audition? Do you think Ms. Werner really likes him best already?" Benny stopped and looked at his fingers. "That was actually three questions." He shrugged.

Jessie smiled. "Three important questions."

"You're right, Benny," Henry said. "The Wundermutt audition mystery is getting even more mysterious."

CHAPTER 4

The Top Three

It was time for a short break.

The Aldens decided to get to know the other dog owners a little better. They went to talk to Dante first.

"Good luck in the next round," Jessie said.

"Thanks," Dante said. "You, too." Dante was acting nervous. He kept glancing over at the door.

"What kind of dog is Buffalo?" Benny asked.

"Ummm." Dante scratched his chin.

"A spotted one. Look, I gotta go some-where." He tugged Buffalo away quickly and left the room.

"Dante sure was in a rush to get out of here." Violet said. "Maybe we can get to know him better later."

Mr. Benjamin was in the corner of the room, brushing Ninja's teeth. The Aldens walked over to him.

"Hello, Mr. Benjamin," Henry said. "Congratulations on the audition so far."

"There is no need to congratulate me," Mr. Benjamin said, standing up. "I knew Ninja would be picked." He tucked Ninja's toothbrush in his pocket. "I'm sorry for you kids, though. *Your* dog doesn't have a chance."

Henry didn't want to seem rude, so he just said, "Ninja is a very good actor."

"The best," Mr. Benjamin said. "It's so wrong that we had to come here to Greenville."

"Greenfield," Benny corrected.

"Whatever," Mr. Benjamin said. "Ninja never has to try out for a role. He is always given everything that he wants!" Mr. Benjamin gathered Ninja's leash. "We are off to buy Ninja a bottle of water in the mall's food court. Ta ta."

The Aldens were alone in the big room.

"I'm so nervous," Violet said. "Mr. Benjamin seems confident that Ninja will win. But I really hope that Watch will get the best score," she said. "Then he'll be a star."

"And Josh will get his bike fixed," Henry put in.

"Josh can bring his bike when he visits us in Hollywood!" Benny said.

Just then Grandfather came into the audition room. "I met Ms. Werner outside," he said. "She said you had a short break, so I came to take you out for a snack." He gave Benny a wink. "How is everything going?"

"Great! Watch has been picked to go to the next part of the audition," Jessie said.

"He's going to be famous," Benny said. "When Watch is a superstar, you can be his chauffeur so you'll drive him to all his important meetings," Benny explained.

"We'll even get you a fancy hat!"

Grandfather laughed.

After a snack and a short walk, Grandfather dropped the children and Watch back at the audition room. He made plans to pick up them up when it was over later.

"You see, I'm already the chauffeur," he said.

After Grandfather was gone, Henry saw something odd through the big window at the back of the room.

Ms. Werner and Dante were outside speaking privately. It looked like Ms. Werner was giving Dante a marker pen. But he wasn't sure. "Did you see that?" Henry asked Jessie.

"I think I saw Ms. Werner give Dante a marker," Jessie said.

"That's what I thought, too!" Henry said.

"That's really weird. A bunch of strange things have happened at this audition," Jessie said.

"You should write it all down in your journal when we get home," Henry said.

"Yeah," Jessie agreed. She began thinking

about what she'd write. She'd start with the fact that none of the dogs in line were eating the Wundermutt food. Except Buffalo.

"Hello." Lisa came over to the children. "Your dog is terrific."

Jessie beamed. "Thanks," she said.

"Is it fun to work in show business?" Benny asked.

Lisa didn't smile. "No. I don't think it's fun."

"Why not?" Benny asked. "I think it would be great!"

Lisa groaned. "It might be great for some people. But I don't want to be in show business. I want to do other things for the Wundermutt Company."

"What do you want to do?" Violet asked in her soft voice.

"I'm an inventor," Lisa told the children. "I've created a new dog training product. It's called—"

"Lisa, I need your help," said Ms. Werner, who had come back into the room.

"I have to go now." Lisa sighed. "But I have

a plan." She tossed back her hair and gave a small smile. "Soon everyone will notice me and listen to my incredible idea!" With that, Lisa hurried off.

"What do you think she has in mind?" Henry wondered.

* * * *

It was time for the obstacle course. Lisa showed the dogs and owners how it worked. "Each dog will have to go over the log, under the bench, through the hoop, and finally, slip down the slide," she said.

"We want to see how athletic and healthy your dog is," Ms. Werner said. "Plus, these same tricks will be used in the commercial."

Ms. Werner pointed at Lisa's clipboard. "We will give each dog points for how well they perform on each of the events we have planned. At the end, the dog with the most points will get to go to Hollywood, star in the Wundermutt commercial, and win one hundred dollars in prize money."

"Wow!" Jessie said. "That's exactly enough

to get Josh's bike fixed."

"Winning is going to be a piece of cake!" Benny exclaimed.

"Benny's always thinking about food," Henry said with a laugh.

Ms. Werner announced that Buffalo would run the course first. Ninja would be next, and finally, Watch.

Buffalo moved up to the starting line. A bell rang and Buffalo started out. The dog jumped smoothly over the log, though his back feet briefly touched it.

As Buffalo went through the course, Dante cheered him on.

"Good dog!" he shouted. "Don't mess up. No mistakes. People are counting on you. When you win this audition, it'll prove a point."

When Buffalo slid under the bench, he hit the underside with his back. The bench wobbled but didn't tip. Buffalo sailed through the hoop, but skidded on his landing. For the last trick, Buffalo slid smoothly down the slide.

At the finish line, Dante gave Buffalo a big hug. "Good job, Bandit!" he said. "Great work."

"Bandit?" Benny whispered. "I thought his dog's name is Buffalo."

"I don't know why he called his dog another name," Henry said.

"We must have heard wrong," Violet said.

"All of us?" Jessie asked.

"Great work, Buffalo." Ms. Werner said. "A solid run." She told Dante he didn't need to stay to watch the others.

"Buffalo needs to be refreshed," Dante said. Then they headed out.

When Mr. Benjamin moved Ninja to the start line, Benny began to clap. "Go, Ninja!" he said. He still wanted Watch to win, but it was exciting to see his favorite TV hero in action. "Now, Ninja, now!" he shouted. That was what the announcer on "Ninja at Night" said whenever Ninja sprang into action.

But Mr. Benjamin wasn't pleased. He just glared at Benny.

"Sorry," Benny said, and then he was quiet.

The bell sounded and Ninja was off. He went over. Under. Through and down. Unlike Buffalo, Ninja didn't need any direction on the course. He did it all perfectly on his own.

"Good job, Ninja," Benny said softly when Ninja's turn was over.

"Ninja really did well," Henry admitted. "He's a pro."

"I told you Ninja would win," Mr. Benjamin said, as Ninja sat down next to his feet.

Watch was getting ready to take his turn on the obstacle course.

Mr. Benjamin looked around the room. "Hold on," he said. He turned to Ms. Werner. "I can't find Ninja's leash."

Everyone looked around, but nobody noticed the leash.

"I'll check over by the stage kitchen," Henry said. Lisa went to look with him. Jessie and Benny said they'd look by the door and under the waiting area chairs.

"I'll check the little office," Violet told them, and Ms. Werner followed her. The desk was messy. Violet picked up a coffee mug so she could move some papers. On one side of the mug was a picture of a white fuzzy dog. There was a big red heart around the dog. On the other side there was some writing.

"I'll take that!" Ms. Werner said. She was right behind Violet.

Ms. Werner took the cup so fast that Violet didn't have time to read the writing.

"That dog looked familiar," Violet said. "Is that a photo of a famous dog?"

"No," Ms. Werner said, putting the cup away in a cabinet. "But I wish he was."

Violet looked around the desk. "No leash here."

"I found it!" Benny suddenly called out. "It was under one of the chairs," he said.

Without saying thanks, Mr. Benjamin took the leash. He hooked up Ninja and quickly left the room.

"Okay, Watch," Jessie said, stepping onto the starting line for the obstacle course. "Do your best." She scratched Watch on the neck and set him free.

Brinnnnggg! The bell sounded. Watch was off and running.

Watch went over the log easily, but as he appeared on the other side there was a loose bit of rope tangled around his leg.

"Where did that come from?" Henry asked.

Watch managed to remove the rope himself by shaking one of his hind legs. He then hurried to the next task. As he ran beneath the bench, one of the four legs suddenly came off! The bench tipped over and narrowly missed falling on him. When Watch jumped through the hoop, it broke in two.

"Something bad is going on," Violet said.

The final task was the slide. Watch got up the steps okay, but as he began to slip down, the whole slide began to shake. It wobbled. Then it creaked. It was beginning to fall over!

"Oh no!" Jessie said. She lunged towards Watch to grab him. She had him in his arms just before the whole slide collapsed with a loud and heavy *clomp*. Henry, Violet, and

Benny rushed over. Ms. Werner and Lisa hurried over, too.

"Is he all right?" Ms. Werner asked, very concerned.

"He's fine," Benny reported after giving Watch a big hug.

"I'm glad he's okay," Ms. Werner told the children. She turned to Lisa, "How could that have happened? Did you check the course?"

"It was fine when Ninja and Buffalo went through," Lisa said. "I didn't think I needed to check it again. I really don't know what happened."

"I'm sorry about the slide," Ms. Werner said. She took the clipboard from Lisa and made some notes on the top page. Then she turned to the children, "Watch needs to do better in the next round if he wants to win."

CHAPTER 5

A Dog's Day

There was another short break so everyone could walk their dogs outside. Jessie held on to Watch's leash, leading him to a grassy area near the parking lot.

"I don't get it," Violet told the others. "How is it possible that Watch had so many problems on the obstacle course? None of those things happened when Ninja or Buffalo ran the course."

Henry thought a moment. "This mystery is getting bigger."

"I bet that after we write everything down, it'll all come clear," Jessie said.

"I hope so," Henry replied.

"Wow, look," Benny suddenly said. A big black limousine was pulling into the parking lot.

Mr. Benjamin and Ninja, Dante, and Buffalo came over to see what was going on.

"That limousine must be for Ninja," Mr. Benjamin said.

"No," Ms. Werner said coming up behind them with Lisa. "It's not Ninja's."

Benny pointed and asked Violet, "Do you think someone famous is inside?"

"We'll see," Violet said.

A chauffeur got out of the front of the limousine. He was wearing a flat black chauffeur's hat, just like the one Benny wanted to get Grandfather. The chauffeur opened the limo's side door. A teenaged boy with blonde hair and dark sunglasses got out.

"I know who that is!" Jessie said. "That's Timmy Moore!"

"Isn't he on that skateboarding show?" Henry asked.

"'The Happy Gang,'" Violet added. "I love that TV show!"

"He's really famous," Benny said.

"Timmy likes to be called TM," Jessie said. "I read it online."

"Now, I've seen Ninja and TM all in one day," Benny said happily.

"Timmy is going to be in our Wundermutt commercial," Lisa told them. "He came here to help pick the dog he'll be working with."

"I'm so excited to meet your dogs," Timmy told the dog owners. He gave Benny a thumbs-up.

Back in the audition room, brought the dogs and their owners over to the stage kitchen. It had an oven and a refrigerator and even a little table with four chairs.

"Timmy is going to stand here," Ms. Werner said. She pointed to a spot by the counter.

As Timmy walked towards the stage, he stopped to pet Watch.

"That's a handsome-looking dog," he told Benny.

"Thanks." Benny beamed. "It would be great if our dog was in this commercial with you!"

"Yeah," Timmy said. "I'll tell you though, this is going to be my last commercial—ever." He put his hands on his hips. "I'm done with TV and commercials. I want to do movies next—no matter what it takes!" Timmy tossed back his shoulders and stepped onto the stage.

Ms. Werner explained that for this part of the audition, each dog needed to rush into the kitchen and leap into Timmy's arms. Ninja would be going first, then Buffalo, then Watch.

Mr. Benjamin took Ninja to the stage. Right away he began to complain to Ms. Werner.

"Timmy is standing too close to the counter," he said. "He needs to leave room for my dog. Also, the lights over the counter are too bright. Ninja needs red lighting, not blue. His fur looks better in red."

With a sigh, Ms. Werner told Timmy to move and adjusted the lights. "But only because Mr. Lillipool asked me to give special attention to Ninja."

When everything was set, Mr. Benjamin said, "I need complete silence on the set!" He looked at Benny. "You are breathing too loud. Stop it now."

Benny puffed out his cheeks and held his breath.

When Ms. Werner gave the signal, Ninja ran into kitchen and hopped up into Timmy's arms. Timmy caught him easily.

"Good job!" Lisa said. Everyone could see that Ninja did well.

Mr. Benjamin hurried up to the stage where Ninja was. "Sorry we can't stay and see the other auditions," he said. He did not sound very sorry. "But Ninja needs for some beauty rest."

"Be back by nine tomorrow morning," Lisa told Mr. Benjamin. Then she and Ms. Werner went back to the office to make notes. Timmy walked over to corner of the room and made a call on his cell phone.

"It's interesting that Timmy wants to be a movie star," Henry whispered to the other Aldens.

"I sure hope Watch can be in this last commercial with him," Benny said. "But Ninja did really well. Maybe he will get the job."

"Mr. Benjamin seems to think so," Jessie said. She had to keep her voice down. Behind them, Mr. Benjamin was taking his time gathering his things together.

"Watch will do a great job," Violet said.

Finally, Mr. Benjamin and Ninja left.

"Buffalo's turn," Ms. Werner called. But Buffalo was over by the door.

"Um...small problem here. Buffalo needs a quick walk," Dante told Ms. Werner. "Can we let Watch go next?"

"That's fine with us," Jessie said. Ms. Werner agreed. So Dante took Buffalo outside.

Jessie took Watch up on stage and waited.

"Dinner!" Timmy called out. That was the cue for Watch to run into the kitchen and leap toward Timmy. But instead of running to Timmy, Watch ran right past, sniffing the ground. He ran off the stage and went straight to a box tucked in a dark corner of the audition room.

"No, Watch!" Benny called. He ran over and caught Watch by the collar.

"Let's try that again," Ms. Werner said.

Jessie led Watch back to the stage.

Benny covered his eyes with his hands, "Tell me when it's over, Henry," Benny said. "I'm too nervous to look."

Of course, Benny was peeking between his fingers when the scene began. Again, Watch ran right past Timmy and off the stage. He went straight up to the box. He was sniffing wildly.

Just then, Dante came back with Buffalo. "Is it our turn yet?" he asked.

"Yes," Ms. Werner answered. She turned to the Aldens. "I'm sorry. There is no way I can possibly give Watch any points for this part of the audition," she told them.

Lisa spoke up. "There's still tomorrow. Let's hope he does better in the morning." Ms. Werner and Lisa went back to the office to make more notes.

"I can't believe it!" Jessie said. "The other dogs aren't having these kinds of problems."

"Jessie," Benny said. "Something smells funny."

"I don't smell anything," Jessie said, taking a whiff.

"I think Benny means something strange is going on," Henry said. "It sure does seem like bad things keep happening to Watch."

Benny rubbed his belly. "No, Jessie and Henry. This is a real smell. A yummy smell." Benny followed the scent. It led him right up to the same box that Watch had sniffed out.

Benny picked up the box.

"I think my stomach knows what's inside." Benny said. "It's a steak."

Henry opened the box. "You're exactly right, Benny. There is a steak in here!" Jessie got Ms. Werner and Lisa.

"This is the reason that Watch was distracted," Jessie said, pointing at the box. Ms. Werner was surprised. "How did a steak get in here?" She looked at Lisa.

"Don't ask me," Lisa said.

"First there was the broken slide. Now, there's the steak," Jessie said. "It appears that someone doesn't want Watch to win."

"But who?" Violet asked.

"And what should we do?" Henry added.

"I have never run into a problem like this before," Ms. Werner said. She turned to Lisa. "See if you can figure out who might be trying to ruin Watch's audition." Then she thought for a moment, and said, "Watch can have another try, after Buffalo takes his turn."

Dante took Buffalo up to the stage.

"Dinner!" Timmy called out.

Buffalo leapt right into Timmy's open arms. It was a good jump. But when Timmy bent to put Buffalo down, the dog squirmed and knocked Timmy over into the nearby chair. The chair crashed to the floor with a bang.

"Good job," Ms. Werner said, coming over to give Buffalo a pat. "Your dog is a good jumper."

"Thanks," Dante said. He put on Buffalo's leash. "See you tomorrow," he told everyone. Then he and the dog left.

It was almost time for Watch to take his turn again. While Ms. Werner and Lisa talked to Timmy, the Aldens gathered together to talk.

"Watch can jump just as high as Buffalo," Benny told Henry. "And I bet Watch won't knock Timmy down, either."

"It's so odd," Jessie added. "Buffalo's just not that great a performer. And yet, Ms. Werner loves him."

"I know this sounds strange, but I think that Buffalo's speckles keep getting darker," Violet said.

"I have a funny feeling about Dante," Henry added.

"I think we should help figure out who is ruining Watch's audition," Jessie said. "Dante should be our first suspect."

"Our second suspect should be—" Violet began, but she was interrupted by Ms. Werner.

"It is now Watch's turn," Ms. Werner said.

Jessie led Watch to the stage again.

"Dinner!" Timmy called.

On cue, Watch ran. He jumped high— higher than either Buffalo or Ninja had jumped! He soared right into Timmy's open arms. Timmy then set Watch down without any trouble at all.

"Great job, Watch!" Jessie said. Benny, Henry, and Violet applauded. Even Timmy looked impressed.

"That's much better," Ms. Werner said. She did not smile. But she did not frown, either. "But remember, there's still one more day."

"See you tomorrow," Lisa said.

Jessie put Watch's leash back on. The Aldens waved good-bye and walked out through the mall to meet Grandfather. It had been a long day and they were tired. All except for Benny, who was still excited.

"Watch was incredimarzing," Benny said.

"Incredimarzing?" Henry asked.

Benny explained, "Watch was incredible, marvelous, and amazing. All mixed up."

"Incredimarzing!" Henry repeated. He smiled. It was the perfect word.

CHAPTER 6

A List of Suspects

After dinner that night, Benny came into the boxcar and plopped onto a beanbag chair.

"Oh good," Jessie said. "We're all here."

"I had to help Grandfather with the dishes," Benny said. "That's the thing about dinner: I like the eating part, but I don't like the cleaning up-after-part."

Henry laughed.

Jessie opened a new page in her notebook. At the top of the page she wrote:

"The Wundermutt Audition Mystery." She underlined it and then wrote: "Suspects."

"Let's get started. I think we should make a list of people who we think might be trying to ruin the audition. I already put Dante on the list because there is so much strange stuff going on with him. Who should I write down next?" she asked.

"I think Mr. Benjamin should be second. He isn't very nice," Violet replied.

Yes. Mr. Benjamin is a very big suspect," Jessie said. "Before dinner, I did a little Internet research about Ninja. I printed this out." She handed Henry a piece of paper.

Henry read it. "It's a news story. It says that 'Ninja at Night' has been cancelled," he said.

"Oh no!" Benny said. "This is the worst news ever."

Henry read on. "This story says that the show was cancelled because of Mr. Benjamin. No one likes him. He's always demanding expensive, fancy stuff for his dog."

Jessie shrugged. "I guess the TV people got tired of working with Mr. Benjamin. If Mr. Benjamin is mean to people, it doesn't matter if Ninja is a good actor or not."

"I wonder if Mr. Benjamin is trying to get rid of Watch, so Ninja will get the commercial job for sure," Violet said.

"But why isn't he trying to get rid of Buffalo, too?" Benny asked.

"Maybe Mr. Benjamin doesn't think Buffalo is good enough to win," Henry replied.

"That makes sense. Mr. Benjamin might be the one, but it might also be Lisa who is wrecking things." Jessie paused. "Maybe even Mr. Lillipool." Then she added, "Of course, it might be Timmy."

"Well," Henry laughed. "I think that list covers almost everyone we met today."

"Except Ms. Werner," Jessie added. "Should we write her down too?"

"I don't know," Violet said. "She hasn't done anything too weird—yet."

"Except giving Dante a marker and acting

like Buffalo's biggest fan," Henry said to Violet.

"Oh," Violet said. "That reminds me. Ms. Werner had a coffee mug with a photo of a white fluffy dog on it. Ms. Werner seems to like white fluffy dogs."

"But Buffalo has speckles," Benny said. "She likes fluffy white dogs and fluffy speckled ones too."

"I think we better put Ms. Werner on the list," Henry said. "Just in case."

Jessie wrote some more. "Okay. I got them all down," she said. "Now we need to write the reason that each one is a suspect. Mr. Benjamin is the easiest. He wants to win a new job for Ninja."

"For Ms. Werner, write down that she's is so enthusiastic about Buffalo even though that dog just isn't very good," Henry said.

"I think that Dante really wants Buffalo to get the commercial," Violet added. "Don't forget that he's the only dog who ate the food," Benny added.

"Always thinking of food, huh, Benny?"

Jessie said with a chuckle. "You know, eating the food's not a bad thing. The dogs are supposed to eat the food."

"Buffalo is still the only one who has eaten the food," Benny said.

"Okay, Benny. I've got it," Jessie said, writing quickly. "I also put down Buffalo's speckles. There's something about those speckles that make me wonder."

"Let's talk about Lisa," Henry said. "She told us she had a plan to get attention. Maybe she's ruining the audition just to get noticed."

"She said she was an inventor," Benny said. "What's she up to?"

"I don't know," Jessie said. Jessie stuck a question mark next to Lisa's name on the list.

"Hmm. What about Timmy Moore?" Violet asked.

"That's right!" Jessie said. "He told us this was his last commercial because he wants to be in movies. Maybe Timmy thinks he will get a good movie part if he works with the famous dog, Ninja."

"First you tell me that 'Ninja at Night'

is cancelled, now you think that Timmy is wrecking Watch's audition?" Benny put his head in his hands. "It's too horrible to think about!"

Henry came over to Benny and sat next to him on the floor. "We don't know if Timmy is making the problem, Benny. We're just making a list. We're brainstorming."

Benny's head popped up, "Wow, that's exactly how the inside of my brain feels. Like there's a storm going on in there!"

"Okay," Jessie said, as she finished writing. "I have everyone." Jessie planned to carry the list with her while they searched for more clues.

"Look, here comes Josh," Henry said. Josh Greene had come into the backyard to return Henry's bike.

"How did the audition go?" Josh asked. He bent to pet Watch.

"Watch did really well," Benny said. "Except for the slide and the steak."

The Aldens told Josh the whole story.

"Someone is trying to ruin the audition

for Watch," said Jessie. "And we are going to find out who it is."

"And if Watch wins, you'll be able to get your bike fixed," Benny told Josh.

"That's right, the prize is a hundred dollars!" Henry added.

"That would be great!" Josh said and stood up. "I hope you figure it all out. Good luck," he said. He waved good-bye and left.

Grandfather came out to the boxcar. "You'd better come inside. It's late and you have a busy day tomorrow," he said. "Watch is already asleep, probably dreaming about his audition."

"But we can't go to sleep yet," Benny said. "We didn't solve the mystery." Benny yawned.

"Tomorrow is a new day," Grandfather told them. "Maybe everything will come clear in the morning."

"I sure hope so," Jessie said. The others nodded.

CHAPTER 7

The Final Day

In the morning, Grandfather dropped the children and Watch off at the Green-field Mall. Day Two of the Wundermutt commercial audition was about to begin.

"Hello," Lisa said. She bent over Watch and asked, "Are you ready for a fresh start?"

Watch happily licked her hand.

Jessie held the suspect list and a red pen. "Um, Lisa," she said. "I have a quick question." Jessie clicked open her pen. "Yesterday you said you were an inventor. Is your invention a secret?"

"It's not a secret," Lisa said. "But no one ever asks me about it. Thanks for being interested." Lisa smiled and her eyes lit up. Yesterday she had often seemed to be in a bad mood. But not now.

"I created a new kind of pet repellant," Lisa told them.

"What's that?" Benny said.

"*Repel* means to make something go away," Henry explained.

"Exactly!" Lisa said. "My repellant is a spray that dogs don't like. Sometimes people want to keep their dogs off the furniture. They can spray this on the couch, and the dogs will stay off. I call it 'Get Away Spray.'" Lisa was talking very fast. "I used all natural ingredients in the mixture," Lisa said. "I think this stuff will sell like crazy."

"Sounds interesting," Henry said. "Did you show it to Mr. Lillipool?"

"Oh, gosh, no," Lisa said, shaking her head. "He's too busy and I'm too shy to talk to him." She looked across the room. Mr. Lillipool had just come in.

Violet nodded. She was shy, too.

"If you don't show him, how will he know about it?" Benny asked.

"I gave some of my spray to Ms. Werner," Lisa said. "She said she'd show it to him for me. She told me she has a special meeting with him next week."

Just then, Ms. Werner called across the room. "Lisa, I need your help."

"Gotta go," Lisa said. "I'd give you a sample, but Watch is really well trained. You don't need it." Lisa went to help Ms. Werner.

"Maybe Lisa isn't a suspect anymore," Henry said. "Her big plan wasn't to ruin the audition; it was to get Ms. Werner to have a meeting with Mr. Lillipool."

Jessie crossed out Lisa's name on the list.

Timmy burst into the room. "Sorry, I'm late," he said. "But, you are not going to believe my news! My agent just called. I'm going to be the star of *Lightning Man*! It's a new superhero movie. After this commercial,

I'm going start filming!" Timmy was very happy.

"Wow, Timmy. That is amazing!" Benny said. "I can't believe I'm talking to the star of a new movie!"

Timmy smiled. "I'm going to go tell Mr. Lillipool." He hurried off.

"Timmy's news means that he didn't need to act with Ninja in this commercial to become a famous movie star," Violet said. "He figured out how to get a movie job all on his own."

Jessie crossed Timmy off the suspect list.

Henry looked over Jessie's shoulder at her list. "There are only four suspects left," he said. "Mr. Benjamin, Mr. Lillipool, Ms. Werner, and Dante. Let's watch them carefully."

Ms. Werner announced to everyone that they were ready to begin. "This will be the last part of the audition." She carried two bowls of Wundermutt food. Lisa had a third bowl in her hands.

"Wow!" Benny said, looking at the bowls.

These weren't the plastic bowls they'd used yesterday. These bowls were silver. Each had one of the contestant's names written on it in gold, glittery letters.

"The dogs must each eat a bowl of our Wundermutt food," Ms. Werner explained. "We can't have a commercial starring a dog that doesn't like our food."

Jessie looked at Henry. "I'm worried," she said.

"After the audition is over, the bowls are yours to take home," Ms. Werner told the dog owners. "They are a gift from Mr. Lillipool."

Ms. Werner put down Ninja's and Watch's bowls. Lisa set the food down for Buffalo.

"Do you smell citronella again?" Jessie asked Violet.

Violet sniffed the air. "Yes. Someone around here sure does like that scent," she said.

"Achoo." Benny sneezed. "Achoo!"

Jessie gave Benny a tissue from her pocket.

"I wonder if there is a connection between

the food and the perfume smell," Henry said. "I remember smelling it yesterday around the food, too."

"Maybe," Jessie said. "But I don't know what the connection could be." She took her notebook out of her purse. She wrote on a blank page: *citronella and dog food.*

"It's time for our doggie contestants to eat," Ms. Werner said. "Buffalo will go first."

"No! Ninja will go first," Mr. Benjamin said strongly. He immediately removed Ninja's leash. Ninja trotted right past Dante and Buffalo. He went directly to his bowl of food.

Ninja got to his bowl, sniffed the food, then suddenly turned and walked away. "Must not be hungry," Mr. Benjamin said with a snort. "Ninja eats when Ninja wants to eat."

"You insisted on going first, so if Ninja doesn't eat right now," Ms. Werner said, "he won't get any points for this part of the audition."

"I can't believe you haven't hired Ninja for this commercial already," Mr. Benjamin replied, his voice strained. "He did the best by far in all the other parts of the audition! So what if he won't eat right this second. He's the best dog actor there is. Ninja deserves this part." Mr. Benjamin stomped his foot in anger.

He turned toward the Aldens with an accusing look on his face. "It's those kids," he said, pointing at the Aldens. "They must have done something to Ninja's bowl of food."

"We didn't do anything," Benny replied. "I would never do anything to Ninja. I love his show!"

Jessie put a hand on Benny's shoulder to quiet him. "Mr. Benjamin," she said calmly. "We wouldn't do anything to ruin Ninja's audition."

"Sure you would. Your dog did poorly yesterday, so you need to ruin Ninja's audition today," Mr. Benjamin said. "Your dog can't get over a log or under a bench without messing up. And he toppled the entire slide. Well, that's just bad training." Mr. Benjamin put his hands on his hips. "Your dog didn't deserve to win any points yesterday."

Mr. Benjamin faced Dante. "And *your* dog! Your dog is an even worse actor. He couldn't get through that audition with Timmy, could he? I'll bet he kept running off the stage! Buffalo is a house pet, not an actor."

"But Buffalo didn't run off the stage," Dante said.

"What is Mr. Benjamin talking about?" Benny asked his brother.

"I really don't know," Henry replied.

After insulting Watch and Buffalo, Mr. Benjamin turned back to Ms. Werner. "Bring me a fresh bowl of food and I'll get Ninja to eat it," Mr. Benjamin said.

"It's this bowl or no bowl," Ms. Werner said. "It shouldn't matter what bowl the food's in."

Ms. Werner and Mr. Benjamin stared at each other. They were both angry.

"Wait! I just figured out who's been ruining the audition for Watch!" Henry said.

CHAPTER 8

Henry Explains

Everyone in the room turned toward Henry.

"Really?" Benny asked. "Who has been doing it, Henry? Who? And why?"

Henry walked to the center of the room. Mr. Lillipool and Timmy came over to stand by Ms. Werner, Lisa, and Dante. Mr. Benjamin stood apart from them, but he was also listening to Henry.

"I thought that someone was trying to ruin the audition for Watch," Henry explained.

"But that's not it. Someone wanted to ruin the audition for Watch and another dog. So their dog would win."

"But Buffalo didn't have any problems yesterday. Neither did Ninja," Dante said. "So far only Watch has had the problems."

"I know," Henry said. "But I realized that Buffalo was supposed to go before Watch at the kitchen audition. Buffalo needed a walk, so Watch took his turn instead."

"Oh!" Jessie said. "I get it! You think that the steak was meant to mess up *Buffalo's* audition, not Watch's. Watch already had trouble earlier on the obstacle course."

Mr. Benjamin got all red faced and angry. "I didn't ruin any auditions. Ninja and I weren't even in the room when Watch and Buffalo did their tasks. Both times we left right after we auditioned, before any mishaps took place."

"And that's exactly how I figured it out," Henry said. "Since you weren't there, how did you know that Watch tipped over the bench and broke the slide?"

"Oh my," Lisa said. "How *did* you know those things, Mr. Benjamin?"

"I—" Mr. Benjamin began. Suddenly he pointed at Dante. "That kid told me what happened."

"No, I didn't," Dante said.

"I must have heard it from Ms. Werner then," Mr. Benjamin said.

"No, you didn't hear it from me either," Ms. Werner replied.

"I just realized something else," Jessie told Mr. Benjamin. "You said that Buffalo couldn't stay on stage long enough to finish the kitchen audition. You thought Buffalo went after the steak. But Buffalo went out for a walk. You didn't know that it was Watch who got distracted by the steak instead."

"I—" Mr. Benjamin didn't know what to say.

"I've heard enough," Mr. Lillipool said. "Mr. Benjamin, you have behaved badly. Wundermutt Company will no longer consider Ninja to be a contestant for the commercial."

"You all see that my dog is the best. I was just making sure you knew it!" Mr. Benjamin said.

Benny said softly to Ninja, "No matter what Mr. Benjamin did, you're still my hero." The black Lab wagged his tail.

Mr. Lillipool shook his head. He pointed to the exit.

"Hmph! Ninja will be a star again. Just you wait and see!" Mr. Benjamin told them. He put on Ninja's leash and stomped out of the room.

Mr. Lillipool came over and shook Henry's hand. "Good detective work, young man," Mr. Lillipool said.

Henry pointed at his brother and sisters and said, "The Aldens work together as a team."

Mr. Lillipool shook hands with Violet, Jessie, and Benny. He even shook Watch's paw. "Tell you what," he said. "Let's forget about yesterday. We'll have both Watch and

Buffalo eat a bowl of Wundermutt food. It'll be a race. Whoever finishes his bowl first, wins the audition. Agreed?"

The Aldens all nodded their heads yes. Dante's eyes opened wide, then he also nodded his head in agreement.

"Come on, Watch," Benny said. He guided Watch over to the bowl with his name on it. "This is your favorite food."

Dante took Buffalo to his bowl.

"On your marks," Mr. Lillipool said.

"Get set," Lisa said.

"Go!" Ms. Werner said. Then, the eating race began. Buffalo dove into his bowl, chomping loudly.

"Eat up, Watch," Benny told the dog. Watch poked his nose in the bowl. But then, just like Ninja had done earlier, he turned and walked away. Watch was more interested in Buffalo's food than his own. Jessie had to hold his collar to bring him back to his own bowl.

"What's wrong with Watch?" Benny asked.

"He must be nervous," Violet said.

Jessie bent down and said, "Relax and eat, Watch."

Watch refused. Buffalo kept on eating.

"Watch should be super hungry," Benny said. "I mean, we've been here a whole hour already. I know that I'm so hungry, I could eat a bear!" Violet took a turn getting Watch up to his bowl.

"Something's wrong," Violet said. "Why won't Watch eat?"

"I don't know," Henry replied. "But now Buffalo is more than halfway done. It looks like we're not going to go to Hollywood."

Benny frowned. "But I wanted to get Grandfather a chauffeur's hat," he said.

"Josh won't get his bike fixed, either," Violet said sadly.

"The audition is over," Ms. Werner suddenly announced. "Buffalo just finished his last bite of Wundermutt food. Buffalo is the winner of the Wundermutt Food Commercial!"

CHAPTER 9

Who is Buffalo?

I'm so sad," Benny said.

Henry put his arm around his little brother. "Watch did his best. I think its time to find Grandfather and head home," Henry said,

"Hot chocolate would make me feel better," Benny said. "And maybe we could get a bone for Watch. He did do his best." Benny gave Watch a hug.

"Sure thing," Jessie said.

Violet put the leash on Watch. "Good try, boy," Violet said.

The kids shook hands with Mr. Lillipool, then went over to congratulate Dante.

"Good luck in Hollywood," Henry said.

"Yeah," Dante said, shuffling his feet and not looking up.

"Aren't you excited about going?" Benny asked. "I would be jumping up and down."

"I'm not going to Hollywood," Dante said. "Just Buffalo. I get to keep the money, though." He shrugged and said, "But I'm not sure I deserve it."

"Why don't you get to go to Hollywood with your dog?" asked Benny.

"Why don't you think you deserve the money?" Jessie asked.

Dante stumbled over his answers. "Oh, well, you know, Hollywood's far away and well, really, Ban—I mean Buffalo—did all the work. I just showed up. So, um, well, bye now." Dante replied. Then he waved awkwardly and headed over to Ms. Werner.

"Hmm," Henry said, "Even though we solved the mystery, there's still something weird here."

"Henry, can we head out now?" Benny asked.

"Sure, Benny," Henry replied. "Let's go."

On the way out, they walked past the obstacle course.

"Seeing that obstacle course makes me really mad at Mr. Benjamin," Benny said. "He shouldn't have cheated." The Aldens all agreed.

The kids walked past Timmy in the stage kitchen. He was near the refrigerator, reading his lines for the commercial.

He waved at the Aldens and said, "Sorry you aren't coming to Hollywood. But I'll send you free tickets to see Lightning Man when it comes out."

"Thanks," Jessie replied. She was holding Watch's leash, leading him towards the exit.

"Don't forget your souvenir bowl," Lisa said to the Aldens. She pointed at the silver bowl.

"I'll go get the bowl," Henry said. "I'll meet you by the door."

Henry walked back into the audition

area. He saw that Ms. Werner was hugging Buffalo. Dante was standing a bit back from them. "Way to go," Henry heard her say in a very low voice. "We showed them, didn't we?" Straightening up, she said, "I bet you are still hungry, you good doggie, you." Picking up Buffalo's bowl, she filed it with more Wundermutt food, then set it back down.

"That's another odd thing," Henry said to himself. "Ms. Werner loves that dog too much."

Henry picked up Watch's bowl. It was still full of food. He carried it over to his siblings.

"I smell that citronella perfume again," Violet said.

Benny sneezed.

Suddenly, Watch made a big tug on his leash. Jessie lost control. Watch dashed across the audition room. His nose was tight to the floor.

"Does he smell another steak?" Violet asked.

Benny gave the air a big smell and his

stomach a pat. "Nope. There's no steak here today," Benny replied.

"Then what is going on!?" Jessie asked.

The Alden children ran to catch up with their dog.

Watch was fast. He skidded past Ms. Werner, Buffalo, and Dante.

Watch jumped onto the obstacle course set. He leapt over the log and under the bench. Through the hoop and down the slide. Then Watch flew into the stage kitchen where Timmy was and bounded into his arms. Timmy was surprised, but he was able to catch Watch and then set him down.

Then Watch went straight to the new bowl of food that Ms. Werner had set down for Buffalo. He stuck his nose in the bowl and began eating away.

"Wow!" Benny said. "I told you he was hungry."

Henry, Jessie, and Violet were surprised to see Watch eating out of Buffalo's bowl.

Henry still had the bowl of food with Watch's name on it in his hand.

Mr. Lillipool, Timmy, and Lisa came over to see what was going on.

"He does like my food!" Mr. Lillipool said. Watch continued to gobble up the food.

"Of course," Benny replied. "Wundermutt is all he ever eats at home."

"Then why didn't he eat it during the audition?" Mr. Lillipool asked. "Watch acted like he was repelled by the food."

Henry snapped his fingers. "That's it! He was *repelled*," Henry said. He turned to face Lisa. "Your invention is a big success!"

"And the dog food mystery is now completely solved," Jessie said.

CHAPTER 10

The Smell of Success

"Ms. Werner has been spraying Lisa's Get Away Spray on the dog food bowls," Henry told everyone. "The only dog who never had his bowl sprayed was Buffalo."

"What?" Mr. Lillipool said. "Can you please explain what you mean?" Mr. Lillipool asked.

"This morning, Lisa told us that she'd created a new kind of pet training spray – a repellant." Jessie replied.

Benny quickly added, "It's called 'Get Away Spray.'"

"She was too shy to tell you about it herself," Henry told Mr. Lillipool. "But she told Ms. Werner all about the spray. Lisa gave her a sample. And Ms. Werner agreed to help her show it to you. Ms. Werner was going to have a meeting with you to demonstrate it."

Mr. Lillipool then looked over at Ms. Werner. She stared down at the ground, unwilling to meet his eyes.

"You never set up the meeting, did you?" Lisa asked Ms. Werner.

Ms. Werner shook her head. "No. I didn't," she replied.

Lisa sighed. "All my dreams are ruined," she said sadly.

"What does Get Away Spray do?" Mr. Lillipool asked Lisa. "And what does this have to do with Watch not eating my food?"

"It's a repellant. Made of all natural ingredients," Lisa explained. "The spray will keep dogs off furniture. Or out of the garbage. It will even keep a dog from jumping up on you. Basically," she said, "it'll keep a pet away from anything it's sprayed on."

Henry held up Watch's dog food bowl. "Even a bowl of food," Henry said surely.

The instant Henry held up the bowl, Benny sneezed. "Achoo!"

"Yes. My spray will even repel a dog from his own food," Lisa replied.

"Interesting," Mr. Lillipool said. He sniffed the air. "What is that smell? Is it lemon or flowers?" Mr. Lillipool asked.

"Neither," Jessie told him. "It's called citronella."

Mr. Lillipool smelled deeply. "I like it," he said.

"I like it, too," Jessie said. "But it makes Benny sneeze." And just to prove her point, Benny sneezed again.

Mr. Lillipool chuckled. Then said, "Why would Ms. Werner put Get Away Spray on the dog food bowls? On everyone else's except Buffalo's?"

"I have the answer," Jessie said. She ran over to the office area and got Ms. Werner's coffee cup, which was full of water. "Yesterday Violet noticed that Ms. Werner's coffee cup had a picture of a fluffy, white dog on it," Jessie said.

"There was a heart around the photo and some writing on the other side. I didn't have time to read the words yesterday," Violet said.

Jessie turned the cup so everyone could see. On the other side was the dog's name: *Bandit*.

"Bandit," Henry said. "That's what Dante called Buffalo that one time."

To everyone's surprise, Jessie poured the water from the coffee cup onto Buffalo. Buffalo shook. His black spots began to disappear.

"Oh, I get it, Jessie!" Benny said. He looked at the dog. "Hello, Bandit."

"Ms. Werner wanted her dog to win so she had Dante draw spots on him. And they called him Buffalo," Henry said. "That must be why Dante isn't going to Hollywood. It's not really his dog."

"You have it all figured out," Dante said. He spoke quietly, looking only at his feet. "Ms. Werner sprayed the Get Away Spray on all the other dogs' bowls so they wouldn't eat the Wundermutt food. She did everything so that Bandit would win," Dante added.

Mr. Lillipool was surprised. "Ms. Werner, we talked about this already. People who work for the company are not allowed to audition their pets. It's a rule," Mr. Lillipool said.

"It's a bad rule. Completely unfair," Ms. Werner complained. "Bandit is the best dog for the commercial. I had my neighbor, Dante, bring Bandit to show you just how great he is."

"Just because you think something is unfair doesn't mean you can cheat," Jessie told her.

"Cheating isn't nice," Benny said. "Not nice at all."

"You're right, Benny," Dante said. Looking up at Mr. Lillipool, Dante continued. "Ms. Werner and I had a deal that if I helped her, I'd get the prize money. But I now see that it was a wrong thing to do. Watch deserved to win. I feel bad that he didn't."

"Young man, at least you now understand that you did wrong," Mr. Lillipool said. "You know that cheating is not okay and that rules are meant to be followed. I'm not so sure Ms. Werner understands that." Mr. Lillipool pointed at Ms. Werner. "You will come to my office on Monday at eight o'clock sharp. We will then discuss whether or not you still have a job at Wundermutt!"

"My dog deserved to win," Ms. Werner said. "I'll show you how good he is. He'll get a different commercial! For another kind of dog food! He'll be famous!" Then, she marched out of the room with Bandit.

Mr. Lillipool ran his hand over his head. "This audition is a mess," he said.

"There was one good thing that came out of all this," Henry said. "We have proven that Lisa's citronella Get Away Spray works really, really well."

Mr. Lillipool stepped up next to Lisa. "We should talk," he said. "You have a bright future as a pet product inventor. When we get back to Hollywood I want to make a big batch of your Get Away Spray."

Lisa smiled.

Mr. Lillipool turned to look at the Alden children. "You've solved two mysteries today. Amazing!" he said.

Watch nudged Mr. Lillipool in the leg.

"You're amazing too, Watch," Mr. Lillipool told the dog. "And because you are such a good dog, and so well trained—you are going to be in our new Wundermutt commercial. Welcome to Hollywood!"

"Congratulations," Dante said with a big smile. "You all deserve it."

"I knew it!" Benny shouted. He held up his lucky penny for everyone to see. "Watch is going to be a superstar!"

"And Josh will get his bike fixed with the prize money," Henry said.

"Fame and fortune," Jessie said with a smile.

"And a chauffeur's hat for Grandfather," Violet said with a laugh.

"Woof!" said Watch.

* * * *

"Hurry up," Jessie said. "It's almost time!"

Henry brought Watch into the room and sat down.

Grandfather was already in his favorite chair. Violet and Jessie were waiting by the TV.

"I've got snacks!" Benny said. He carried in a bowl of pretzels. "I even brought dog treats for the TV star."

After the auditions, the Aldens and Watch had gone to Hollywood. There, in a real TV studio, Watch performed his tricks. They filmed the Wundermutt Commercial with Timmy Moore.

"Am I late?" Josh Green asked as he rushed into the room. He took off his bike helmet.

"It's on after this," Jessie said.

"Great. I didn't want to miss Watch's big commercial!" Josh said. He leaned over and scratched Watch's head. "Thanks so much for fixing my bike," he told the dog.

"I brought you a thank-you present." Josh handed Watch a new chew toy.

"Shhh," Jessie said. "This is it."

The music began. It was upbeat and snappy.

In the commercial, Watch came running through a field of flowers. He jumped over a log and under a bench. Then, Timmy Moore opened the kitchen door and Watch bounded inside.

"Dinner!" Timmy called. Watch leapt up, higher than ever before, straight into Timmy's open arms.

"Good boy," Timmy said. "Here's a yummy Wundermutt meal for you." Then Watch gobbled up the whole bowl.

Everyone applauded as soon as the commercial was over.

"Watch should be in more commercials!" Josh said.

"Well, after the commercial was done, we all decided that we'd had enough Hollywood excitement," Violet explained. "We wanted to come home."

"I got a great Hollywood souvenir," Grandfather said. "Want to see it?"

"Is it another dog food bowl that smells like citronella?" Josh asked. Henry had told him the whole story of the audition and the two solved mysteries.

"No," Grandfather said with a big grin. "This." He reached beneath his chair and pulled out a chauffeur's hat. Grandfather slipped the hat on. "I'm the official driver for Superstar Watch and his crew."

"Sir, can you please drive us out for ice cream?" Benny asked.

"It would be my pleasure, young Master Benny," Grandfather said, tipping his hat. "Shall we bring the Superstar along for a ride?"

"No," Benny said. "He's busy."

The Alden children looked at their dog.

Superstar Watch was in the kitchen, eating a bowl of his favorite Wundermutt dog food.

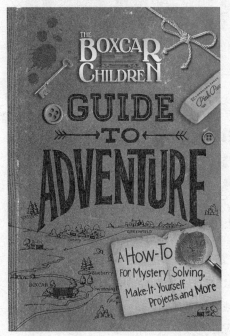

GERTRUDE CHANDLER WARNER discovered when she was teaching that many readers who like an exciting story could find no books that were both easy and fun to read. She decided to try to meet this need, and her first book, *The Boxcar Children*, quickly proved she had succeeded.

Miss Warner drew on her own experiences to write the mystery. As a child she spent hours watching trains go by on the tracks opposite her family home. She often dreamed about what it would be like to set up housekeeping in a caboose or freight car — the situation the Alden children find themselves in.

While the mystery element is central to each of Miss Warner's books, she never thought of them as strictly juvenile mysteries. She liked to stress the Aldens' independence and resourcefulness and their solid New England devotion to using up and making do. The Aldens go about most of their adventures with as little adult supervision as possible — something else that delights young readers.

Miss Warner lived in Putnam, Connecticut, until her death in 1979. During her lifetime, she received hundreds of letters from girls and boys telling her how much they liked her books.